*A Shawnee Legend*

# The Ring in the Prairie

*Edited by John Bierhorst*

*Pictures by Leo and Diane Dillon*

*The Dial Press / New York*

Text copyright © 1970 by John Bierhorst    Illustrations copyright © 1970 by Leo and Diane Dillon
All rights reserved. Library of Congress catalog card number: 70-85546
Printed in the United States of America    First Pied Piper Printing
ISBN 0-8037-7455-9

In a remote part of the forest, where birds and animals were abundant, there lived a young hunter called Waupee, or White Hawk. Tall and manly, with the fire of youth shining in his eye, he walked unafraid through the gloomiest woods, and could follow a track made by any of the numerous kinds of birds and beasts. Every day he would return to his lodge with game, for he was one of the most skillful and celebrated hunters of his tribe.

One day, having hunted farther from home than ever before, he found himself in an open forest where he could see for great distances. Soon there was light breaking through the trees, and before long he came to the edge of a wide prairie covered with grass and flowers.

Walking on, without a path, he suddenly
noticed a ring worn through the sod as if by foot-
steps following a circle.

Yet there was no path leading to it, not the
least trace of footprints. Not even a crushed leaf
or broken twig.

Curious to know the meaning of this strange circle, he hid himself nearby in the tall grass and waited. Presently he heard the faint sounds of music in the air. Looking up, he saw a small object coming down out of the sky. At first a mere speck, it rapidly grew in size, becoming a huge basket filled with twelve sisters of the most enchanting beauty.

As it approached, the music grew plainer and sweeter. When the basket had touched ground, the sisters leaped out and began to dance around the ring. Round and round they went, and as they danced they reached out with sticks to a shining ball in the center of the ring, striking it as if it were a drum.

From his hiding place Waupee gazed upon their graceful motions. He admired them all, but

especially the youngest. At last, unable to restrain himself, he rushed out and attempted to seize her. But the sisters, with the quickness of birds, leaped back to the basket and were drawn up into the sky.

"They are gone," he thought, "and I shall see them no more." He returned to his lodge, but found no rest.

Early the next day he returned to the ring. Not
far from it he found an old stump filled with mice.
Thinking that the sisters would not be frightened
by such tiny creatures, he brought the stump close

to the ring, and changing his form, became one
of them. Soon the sisters came down again and
began to dance.

"Look!" cried the youngest sister. "That stump

was not there before." Frightened, she ran toward the basket. But the others only smiled and gathered round the stump, playfully hitting at it with their sticks. As they did so, the mice, including Waupee, came running out. In a matter of moments the sisters had killed them all—all except one, which was chased by the youngest. As she raised her stick to kill it, the form of Waupee suddenly rose up, clasping her in his arms. The other eleven sprang to their basket and were drawn up into the sky.

Waupee used all the skill he had to please his bride and win her affection. He wiped the tears from her eyes. He told her of his adventures as a hunter, and dwelt upon the charms of life on the earth.

He was tireless in his attentions, picking out the way for her to walk as he led her gently toward his lodge. As she entered it, he felt his heart glow with joy, and from that moment on he was one of the happiest of men.

Winter and summer passed rapidly away, and their happiness was increased by the addition of a beautiful boy to their lodge. But Waupee's wife was a daughter of one of the stars, and as life on the earth began to lose its appeal, she longed to return to her father. She had not forgotten the charm that would carry her up, and took the opportunity, while her husband was out hunting, to construct a wicker basket, which she kept concealed when he was at home. In the meantime she collected such rarities from the earth as she thought would please her father, as well as the most dainty kinds of food.

One day, when all was ready, she went out to the ring, taking her little son with her. They stepped into the basket and she began her song. Carried by the wind, the music caught her husband's ear. It was a voice he well knew. Instantly, he ran to the prairie. But he could not reach the ring before he saw his wife and son rising up. He called out to them, but it was of no use. The basket kept on rising. He watched it till it became a small speck and finally vanished in the sky. He then bent his head down to the ground and was miserable.

Waupee bewailed his loss through a long winter and a long summer. He mourned his wife sorely, but he missed his son even more. In the meantime his wife had reached her home in the stars and had almost forgotten, in her blissful activities there, that she had left a husband on the earth. She was reminded of him only by the presence of her son, who, as he grew up, became anxious to visit the place of his birth.

One day the star said to his daughter, "Go, my child, and take your son down to his father. Ask your husband to come up and live with us. But tell him to bring along one of each kind of bird and animal he kills in his hunting."

Taking the boy with her, the daughter of the star descended once again to the earth. Waupee, who was never far from the ring, heard her voice as she came down through the sky. His heart beat with impatience as his wife and son appeared. Soon they were clasped in his arms.

When his wife had told him of the star's request, Waupee set out with great eagerness to collect the gift. He spent whole nights, as well as days, searching for every beautiful and unusual bird or animal. He preserved only a tail, a foot, or a wing of each, and when everything was ready the family went back to the ring and were carried up.

There was great joy among the stars when they arrived. The star chief invited all his people to a feast, and when they had come together, he announced that they might take whichever of the earthly gifts they liked best.

A strange confusion immediately arose. Some chose a foot, some a wing, some a tail, and some a claw. Those who selected tails or claws were changed into animals and ran off. The others were changed into birds and flew away. Waupee chose a white hawk's feather. His wife and son

did the same, and each one became a white hawk.
Waupee spread his wings and, followed by his
wife and son, descended with the other birds to
the earth, where they are still found to this day.